MAY SAVES THE DAY

BY LAURA GEHL   ILLUSTRATED BY SERENA LOMBARDO

CAPSTONE EDITIONS
a capstone imprint

May Saves the Day is published by
Capstone Editions, an imprint of Capstone
1710 Roe Crest Drive
North Mankato, Minnesota 56003
www.capstonepub.com

Library of Congress Cataloging-in-Publication Data is available on
the Library of Congress website.

ISBN: 978-1-68446-102-8 (hardcover)
ISBN: 978-1-68446-103-5 (eBook)

Summary: May is the founder and sole owner of Word Saver, Inc.
She solves problems on her own. However, when a tornado
threatens the town, May quickly realizes that teamwork may be
the word of the day.

Printed and bound in China.
3322

For Ryan, my partner in marriage, parenting, and life,
with all my love. I couldn't do any of it without you.
—L.G.

To all the little superheroes who will read this.
—S.L.

May loved words so much that she made them her business,
and her phone rarely stopped ringing.

RING! RING!

"Word Saver, Inc. How can I save your day?" May answered.

"THERE'S A SWARM OF ANGRY BEES HEADED FOR THE PLAYGROUND!"

"On my way!" replied May.

May launched a T up into the air . . .

Soon all the kids at the playground had beets.
Except for Stu.

Stu didn't like playing with beets. Stu liked playing with his lasso.

"You're the coolest superhero I've ever seen," Stu said to May.
"Can I be your sidekick? You can call me Lasso Boy."

"I'm not a superhero," May said.
"I'm a successful businesswoman.
And businesswomen do not have sidekicks."

RING! RING!

"Word Saver, Inc. How can I save your day?" May answered.

"A BEAR IS SNEAKING INTO THE SCOUTS' CAMPSITE! HELP!"

"On my way!" replied May.

Arriving at the campground, May spiraled a D toward the bear . . .

The scouts laughed at their leader's new look.
Stu just kept twirling his lasso.

"Are you sure you don't need a sidekick? A lasso-expert sidekick? Every superhero needs a sidekick," he offered.

"I'm not a superhero," May said again. "I'm a small business owner, and I don't have room in my budget for a lasso expert."

RING! RING!

"Word Saver, Inc. How can I save your day?" May answered.

"THERE'S A HUGE SNAKE IN OUR CLASSROOM! HELP!"

"On my way!" replied May.

May carried an E and an R down the school hallway,
straight into Mrs. MacLandon's class . . .

"Who wants to bring home a souvenir?"
May asked, holding up the new sneaker.

All the students waved their hands. All except Stu.
He didn't want a souvenir. He wanted a job.

"Please let me be your sidekick," he begged.
"I can lasso anything! Look!"

"Very nice," May said. "But my business model does NOT
include a sidekick. Do you do web design, by any chance?"

RING! RING!

"Word Saver, Inc. How can I save your day?" May answered.

"THERE'S A RUNAWAY TRAIN! IT'S HURTLING DOWNHILL TOWARD TOWN!"

"On my way!" replied May.

She raced downtown, but . . .

"Looks like you could use some help," Stu said,
showing up at just the right moment.

"Grab the T! Hurry!" May yelled.

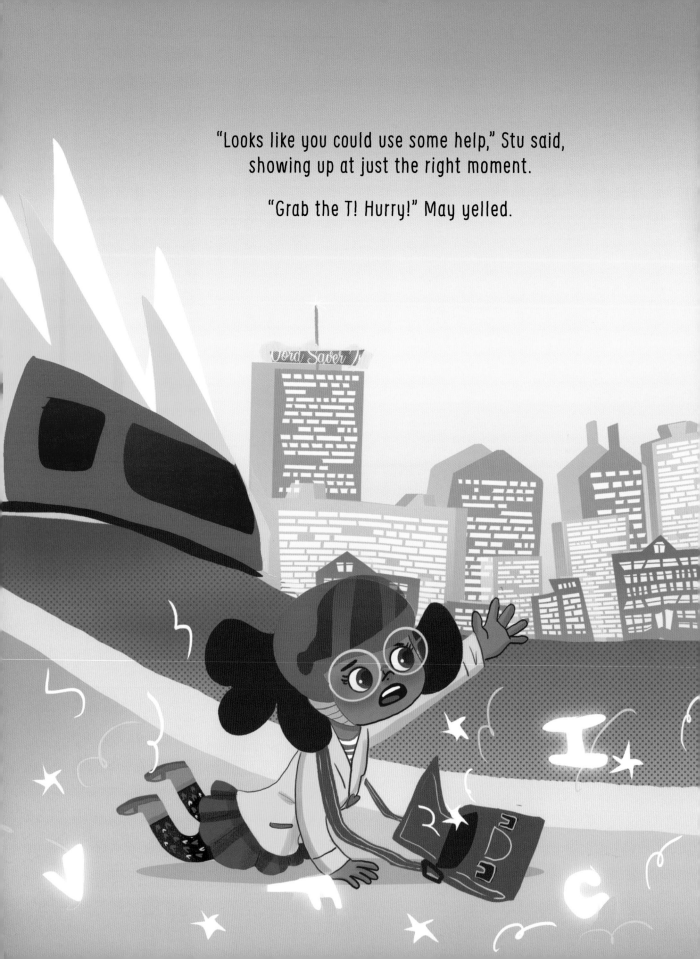

With Stu's help, train became rain.
Everyone was wet but safe.

"Impressive," May told Stu, stuffing fallen letters back into her bag. "You really are a lasso expert."

"Now can I be your . . . wait,
what's that thing in the sky?" Stu asked.

"OH NO! A TORNADO!" May yelled.

May frantically searched through her letters.
"This is a tricky one!"

"It's too windy!" Stu yelled.

"Come on, Lasso Boy, let's work together!" May shouted.
"Can you do a double loop?"

"In my sleep," Stu replied. "Stand back!"

Thanks to their teamwork, the scary tornado
was now just a mess of tomatoes.

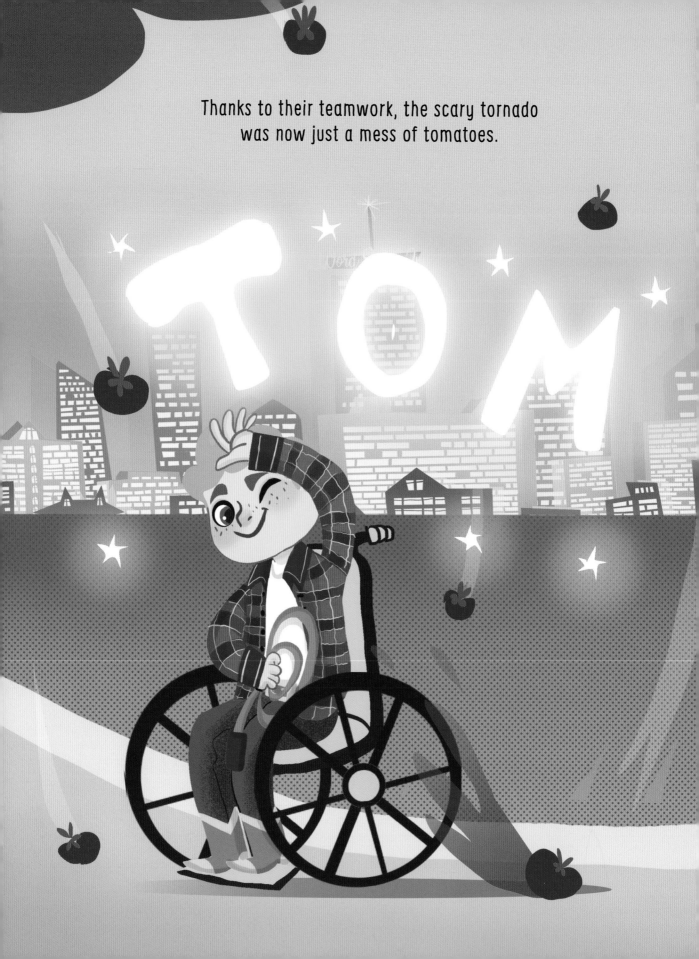

"Well done, kid. Make sure you get cleaned up before you head over to the office," May said. "Businesspeople should look professional. And a tie wouldn't hurt either."

Stu's eyes lit up.
"You mean I CAN be your sidekick?"

"For the last time, I don't need a sidekick!" May said.
"But I could use a partner."

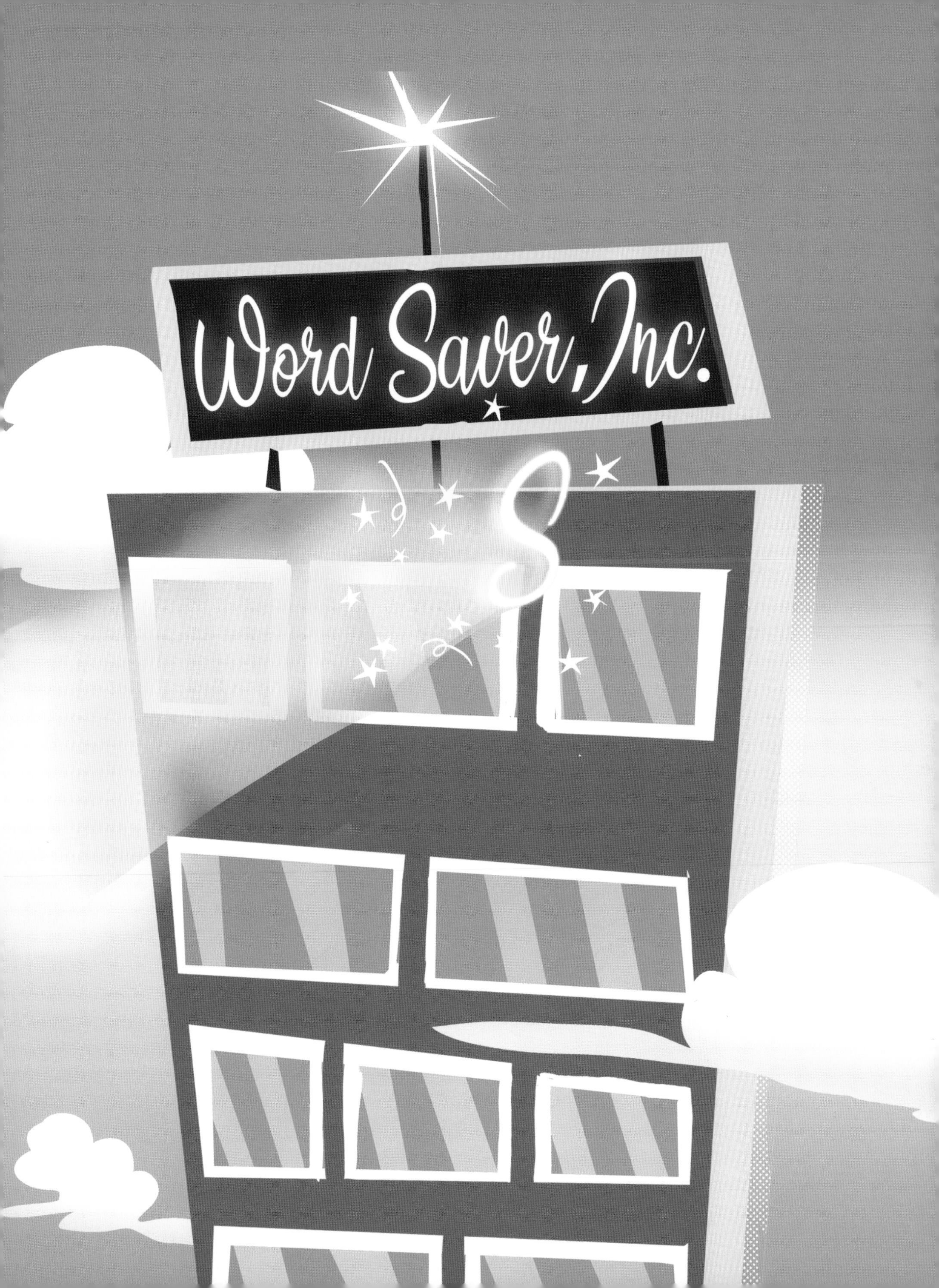
Word Saver, Inc.

"Welcome to the team!"